Maggie's Collection
This book is donated by

David Rochlin

in memory of
Maggie Adler
2007

Mighty Machines

Farm Tractors

by Matt Doeden

Consulting Editor: Gail Saunders-Smith, PhD

Consultant: Kristin Harner
Public Relations/Foundation Director
Minnesota Farm Bureau

Capstone
press

Mankato, Minnesota

Pebble Plus is published by Capstone Press,
151 Good Counsel Drive, P.O. Box 669, Mankato, Minnesota 56002.
www.capstonepress.com

1 2 3 4 5 6 12 11 10 09 08 07

Library of Congress Cataloging-in-Publication Data
Doeden, Matt.
    Farm tractors / by Matt Doeden.
    p. cm.—(Pebble plus: Mighty machines)
    Summary: "Simple text and photographs describe farm tractors, their parts, and what they do"
—Provided by publisher.
    Includes bibliographical references and index.
    ISBN-13: 978-0-7368-6721-4 (hardcover)
    ISBN-10: 0-7368-6721-X (hardcover)
    1. Farm tractors—Juvenile literature. I. Title. II. Series: Pebble plus. Mighty machines.
S711.D585 2007
631.3'72—dc22   2006014717

Editorial Credits
Mari Schuh, editor; Molly Nei, set designer; Patrick D. Dentinger, book designer; Jo Miller,
    photo researcher/photo editor

Photo Credits
Bruce Coleman Inc./Michael Black, 5
Capstone Press/Karon Dubke, cover, 1, 8–9, 10–11
Corbis/Ed Bock, 21
OneBlueShoe, 6–7, 13
Richard Hamilton Smith, 14–15
Shutterstock/Peter Baxter, 16–17
SuperStock/Buck Miller, 19

Note to Parents and Teachers

The Mighty Machines set supports national social studies standards related to science,
technology, and society. This book describes and illustrates farm tractors. The images
support early readers in understanding the text. The repetition of words and phrases
helps early readers learn new words. This book also introduces early readers to subject-
specific vocabulary words, which are defined in the Glossary section. Early readers may
need assistance to read some words and to use the Table of Contents, Glossary, Read
More, Internet Sites, and Index sections of the book.

Table of Contents

Farm Tractors

Tractors are pulling machines.

Farmers use tractors

to pull other farm machines.

Tractor Parts

Tractors have
big bumpy tires.
The bumps help tractors
move across fields.

7

Farmers sit inside

the cab to drive the tractor.

Farmers use

a steering wheel

to turn the tractor.

Tractors have hitches.

Machines hook onto hitches.

Pulling Power

Tractors pull planters
that drop seeds in the field.

Tractors pull sprayers
to kill weeds.

Tractors pull balers
that roll hay.

Mighty Machines

Tractors help farmers

grow crops.

Tractors are mighty machines.

Glossary

baler—a machine that rolls or presses hay into round or square bales

cab—the part of a tractor where a farmer sits

crop—a plant farmers grow in large amounts, usually for food; farmers grow crops such as corn, soybeans, and peas.

hitch—the part of a tractor that other machines hook onto

planter—a machine that drops seeds evenly into rows

sprayer—a machine that sprays and kills weeds

Read More

Nelson, Kristin L. *Farm Tractors.* Pull Ahead Books. Minneapolis: Lerner, 2003.

Randolph, Joanne. *Tractors.* Earth Movers. New York: PowerKids Press, 2002.

Stille, Darlene R. *Tractors.* Transportation. Minneapolis: Compass Point Books, 2003.

Internet Sites

FactHound offers a safe, fun way to find Internet sites related to this book. All of the sites on FactHound have been researched by our staff.

Here's how:

1. Visit *www.facthound.com*

2. Choose your grade level.

3. Type in this book ID **073686721X** for age-appropriate sites. You may also browse subjects by clicking on letters, or by clicking on pictures and words.

4. Click on the **Fetch It** button.

FactHound will fetch the best sites for you!

Index

Word Count: 79
Grade: 1
Early-Intervention Level: 12